Octavia
And Her Purple Ink Cloud

By Donna Rathmell German and
Doreen Rathmell Meredith

Illustrated by Connie McLennan

To the many generations of the Rathmell family:
thanks for all the encouragement—DRG & DRM

For Karla Yaconelli: my sister, my friend, and my
staunchest cheerleader—CM

Library of Congress Control Number: 2005921094
ISBN 13: 978-0-9764943-5-5
ISBN 10: 0-9764943-5-3

Text Copyright © Donna and Doreen Rathmell 2006
Illustration Copyright © Connie McLennan 2006
Creative Minds Copyright © Sylvan Dell Publishing 2006
Text Layout and Design by Lisa Downey
Printed in China

Sylvan Dell Publishing
976 Houston Northcutt Blvd., Suite 3
Mt. Pleasant, SC 29464

www.SylvanDellPublishing.com
Copyright permission: Copyright@SylvanDellPublishing.com

Octavia Octopus lived alone in a small, secret cave in a colorful coral reef. She had many friends, so she was never lonely. She and her friends played a game called "how to hide from a hungry creature."

Octavia clapped all eight arms when Paul Porcupine Fish puffed up to show how he could confuse a hungry creature. He was so big and prickly that Octavia knew Paul would be safe.

Octavia bragged that she could squirt a purple ink cloud to escape. "Watch me!" she said as she squirted . . .

. . . a yellow ink cloud! "Oh no—I'd better practice," she cried.

Octavia laughed when Sandy Seahorse showed how he could hold onto a plant with his tail. He swayed in the water like he was part of the plant. She knew that he would be safe.

Octavia boasted that she could squirt a purple ink cloud to escape. She squirted . . .

. . . an orange ink cloud! "Oh no—I'd better practice," she sighed.

Octavia cheered when Freddy Flounder
changed colors and hid on the ocean floor.
Freddy's eyes went in different directions to
watch all around him.

Octavia explained that she could squirt a
purple ink cloud to escape. She squirted . . .

. . . a green ink cloud! "Oh no—I'd better
practice," she moaned.

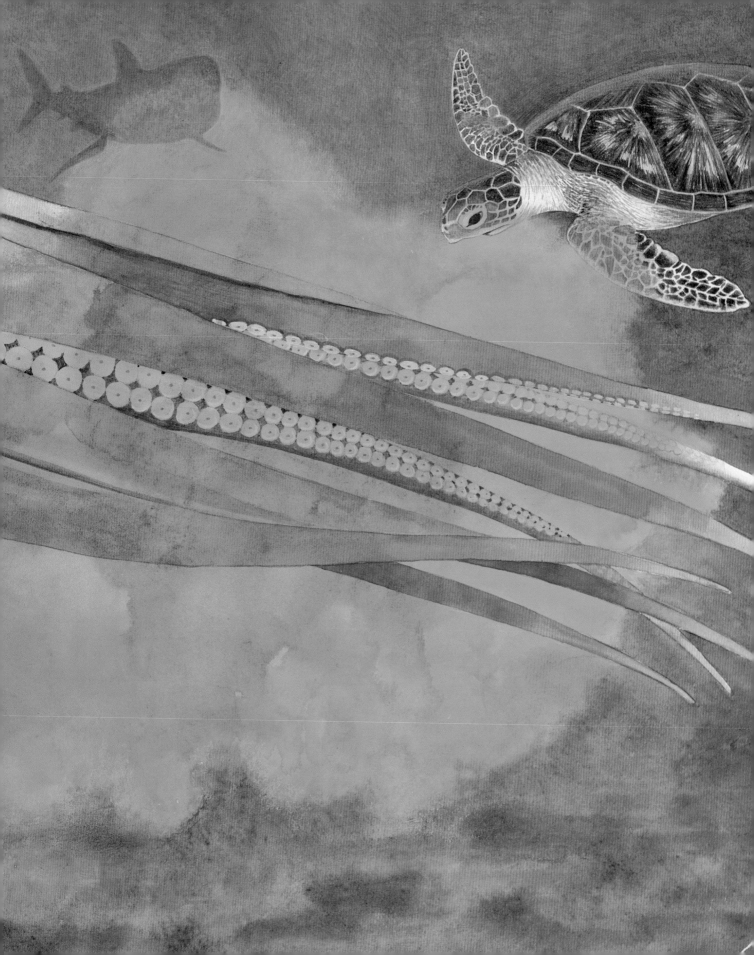

Octavia giggled when Greta Green Sea Turtle
showed how she could hide in the grass. It was hard
to see where she was.

Octavia claimed that she could squirt a purple ink
cloud to escape. She squirted . . .

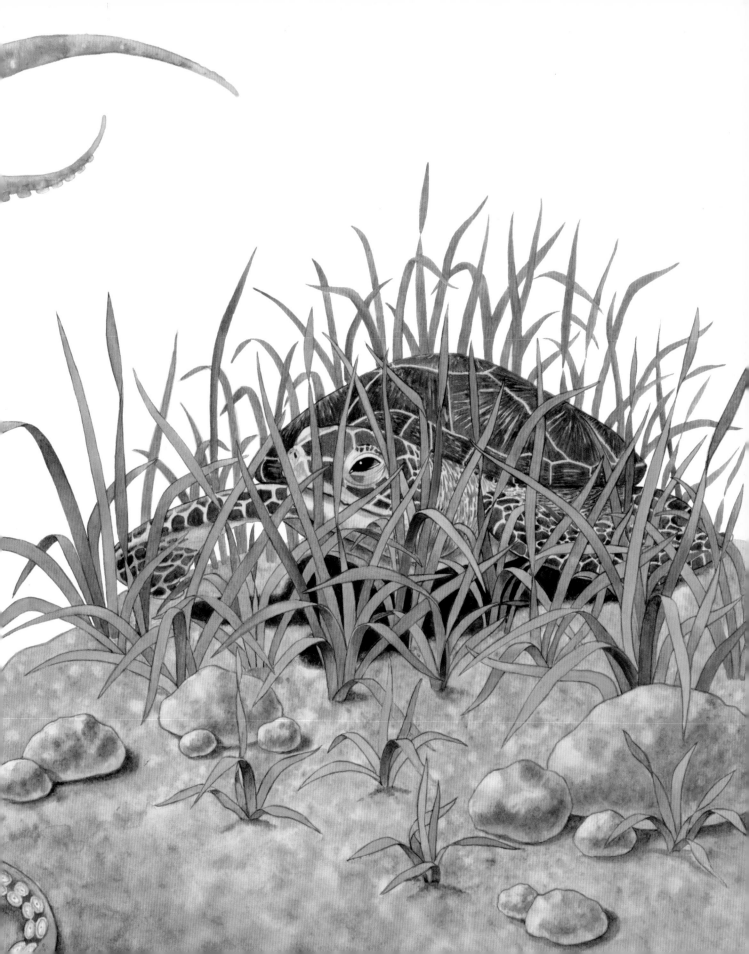

. . . a red ink cloud! "Oh no—I'd better practice," she groaned.

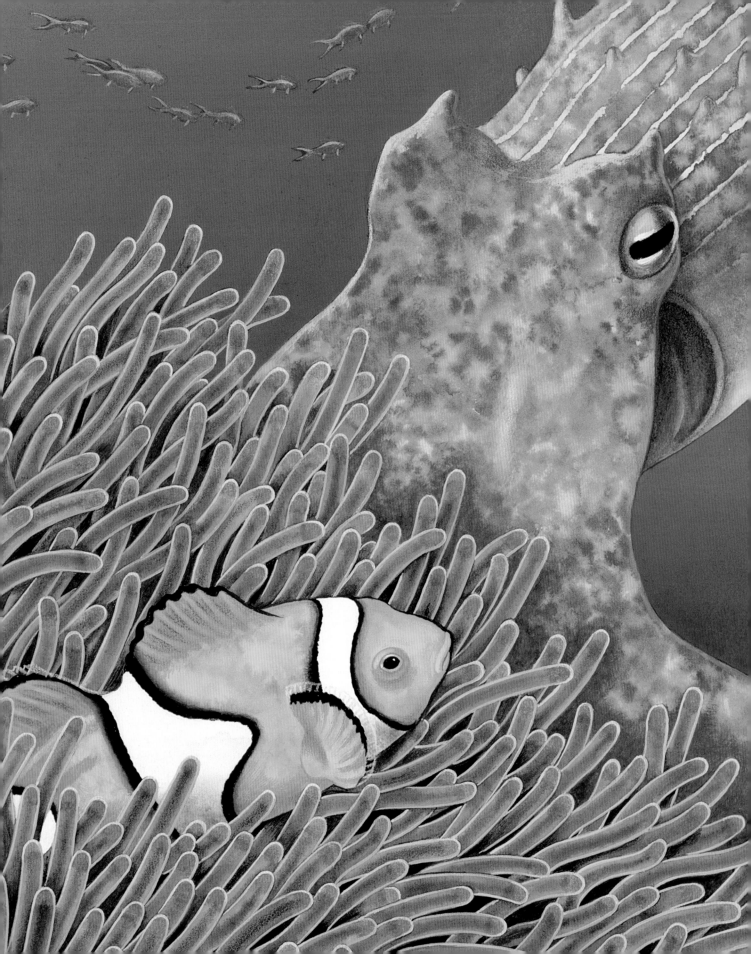

Octavia smiled when Carolyn Clown Fish showed how she could dart into a sea anemone to hide. Octavia knew that the sea anemone's stinging tentacles would help protect Carolyn.

Octavia hoped that she could squirt a purple ink cloud to escape. She squirted . . .

. . . a blue ink cloud! "Oh no—I'd better practice," she whined.

Octavia was jumping up and down as Polly Parrotfish showed how she could hide in holes of the colorful coral reef.

Just then, a great big, hungry shark swam around the reef heading right toward them!

Paul Porcupine puffed up to confuse the shark.

Sandy Seahorse held on tight to the plant.

Freddy Flounder hid on the ocean floor.

Greta Green Sea Turtle hid in the grass.

Carolyn Clownfish darted into the sea anemone.

Polly Parrotfish hid in a small hole in the reef.

Octavia turned white with fright and thought, "I'd better squirt my purple ink cloud so I can swim away!"

She thought very hard and squirted . . .

. . . a great big, dark, purple ink cloud! The shark could not see Octavia as she swam home to her cozy, safe cave.

"Phew," she thought. "It's a good thing I practiced!"

The great big, hungry shark swam away
with an empty belly.

For Creative Minds

Camouflage and Protection

✳ Many animals (land or sea) use camouflage to hide from animals that want to eat them (predators) and animals that they want to eat (prey).

⭐ Some animals like the parrotfish use colors to blend in with their surroundings.

✳ The octopus, flounder, and many other animals can even change the color of their skin to copy the area around them.

⭐ The seahorse hides in plants or coral. Some animals may hide or blend into rocks or sticks.

✳ Sometimes animals just hide in caves or crevices (cracks) or they bury themselves in the sand or mud.

⭐ Animals like the porcupine fish puff up to look bigger than they are.

✳ For protection, animals like crabs and turtles have hard shells; the color of the shells might even help them to hide, too!

⭐ Other animals like jellyfish and sea anemones use stinging tentacles to protect themselves—much like a bee uses its stinger.

Octopus Fun Facts

⭐ An octopus has eight strong arms that it uses for swimming, crawling, fighting, and grabbing prey.

✳ The arms can push and pull and have suction cups (like bathroom plungers or the sticky suction cups on a bath mat) on the bottom to hold onto things.

- If something happens to one of its eight arms, it can grow a new one.

- An octopus lives by itself in a small cave or crevice (crack in rocks or coral) at the bottom of the ocean.

- Sometimes, the octopus "builds" a fence or protective area by placing rocks or shells on top of each other.

- The octopus can remember how to get somewhere and to return to its house.

- The octopus can shoot a stream of water to "clean" out its house or to play with objects.

- It uses a stream of water to swim away from predators quickly.

- The octopus uses very dark red, purple, or black ink clouds to confuse its enemies while it escapes or to catch its prey.

- The octopus can change color to camouflage itself. It can even make patterns on its skin like a checkerboard!

- It turns white when it is scared or red when it is angry – just like many humans.

Octopus Ink Cloud Craft

Copy or download the following page from the Octavia homepage at www.SylvanDellPublishing.com. Using only red, blue and yellow watercolor paints, paint an ink cloud. What colors do you need to mix together to get green, orange, and purple?

OR: Cover the working space with newspaper for easy clean-up. Cut or tear red, blue, and yellow tissue paper (found with wrapping paper) into small strips. Mix a small amount of school glue and water (50/50) and brush onto the "ink cloud" area. Layer the pieces of tissue paper onto the paper. The colors will bleed and blend together. Let dry completely.

Color your
own ink cloud.